Animales pequeñitos / Itty Bitty Animals

RATONCITOS PEQUEÑITOS/ ITTY BITTY MICE

By Jay Moose

Traducción al español: Eida de la Vega

Gareth Stevens Publishing

Please visit our website, www.garethstevens.com. For a free color catalog of all our high-quality books, call toll free 1-800-542-2595 or fax 1-877-542-2596.

Library of Congress Cataloging-in-Publication Data

Moose, Jay.
Itty bitty mice = Ratoncitos pequeñitos / by Jay Moose.
p. cm. — (Itty bitty animals = Animales pequeñitos)
Parallel title: Ratoncitos pequeñitos
In English and Spanish
Includes index.
ISBN 978-1-4339-9912-3 (library binding)
1. Mice — Juvenile literature. I. Title.
QL737.R6 M66 2014
599.353—dc23

First Edition

Published in 2014 by
Gareth Stevens Publishing
111 East 14th Street, Suite 349
New York, NY 10003

Editor: Ryan Nagelhout
Designer: Nicholas Domiano
Spanish Translation: Eida de la Vega

Photo credits: Cover, p. 1 Stockbyte/Thinkstock.com; pp. 5, 7, 11, 19, 23, 24 (nest, tail) iStockphoto/Thinkstock.com; p. 9 Dr. Morley Read/Shutterstock.com; p. 13 © iStockphoto.com/karlbarrett; pp. 15, 24 (pup) Chris Lishman/Flickr/Getty Images; pp. 17, 24 Kirsanov Valeriy Vladimirovich/Shutterstock.com; p. 19 Richard Boll/Photographer's Choice/Getty Images; p. 21 Digital Vision/Thinkstock.com; p. 24 (nest, tail) iStockphoto/Thinkstock.com.

Printed in the United States of America

CPSIA compliance information: Batch #CW14GS: For further information contact Gareth Stevens, New York, New York at 1-800-542-2595.

Contenido

Contents

¡Los ratones son animales diminutos!

Mice are tiny animals!

Tienen una cola larga.

They have a long tail.

Salen mucho
por la noche.

They move around a lot
at night.

Viven en nidos.

They live in nests.

Las mamás ratonas cuidan de sus bebés.

Mother mice take care of their babies.

Los bebés ratones
se llaman crías.

Baby mice
are called pups.

Los bebés son casi siempre rosados. ¡No tienen pelo!

The babies are often pink. They don't have any hair yet!

¡Algunos ratones pueden ser mascotas!

Some mice can be kept as pets!

La gente no quiere a los ratones silvestres dentro de casa. Los consideran una plaga.

Wild mice are not wanted inside houses. These are called pests.

A veces se usan ratones en pruebas de laboratorio. ¡Algunos ratones han ido al espacio!

Mice are sometimes used for tests. They have gone to space!

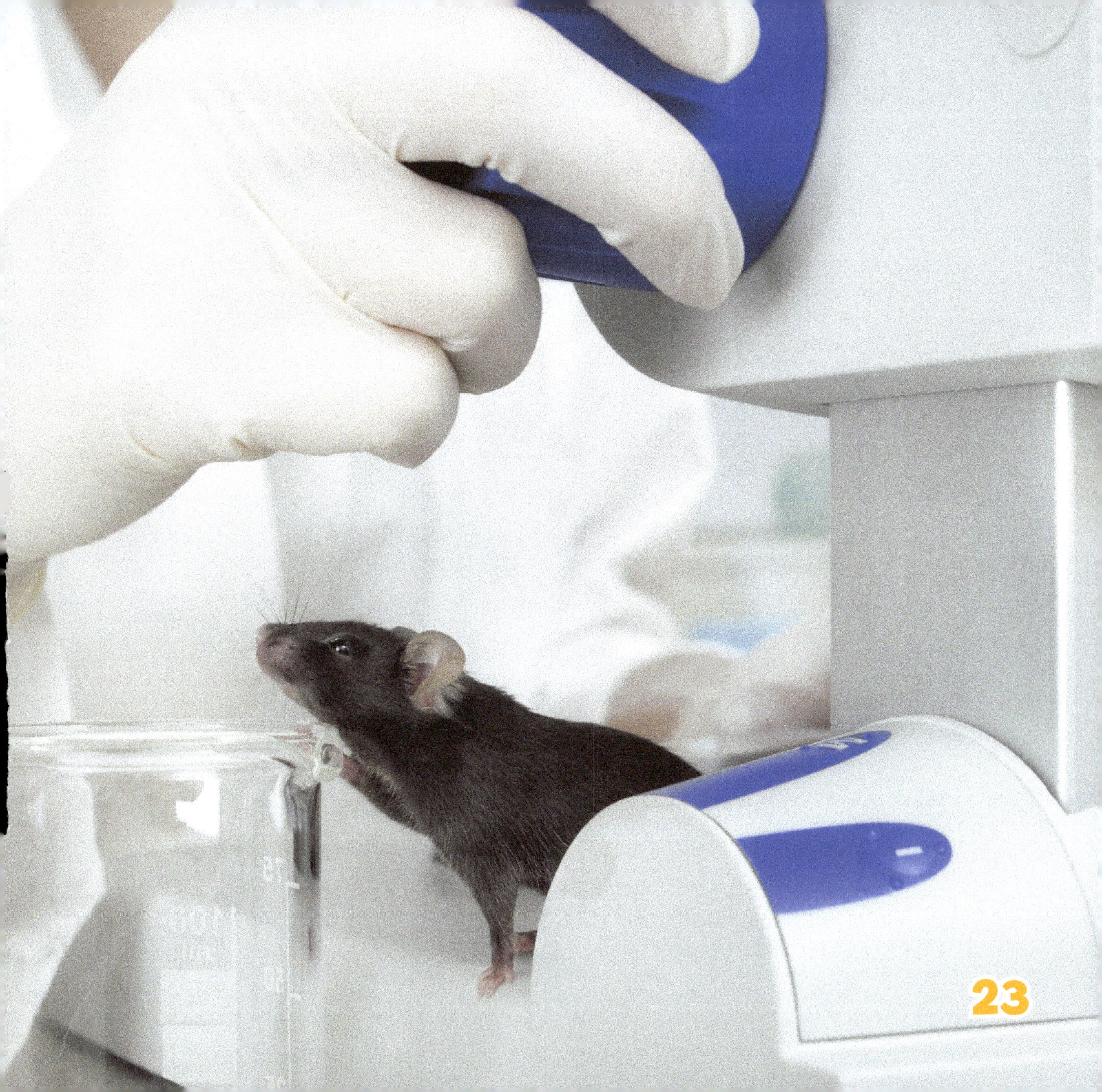

Palabras que debes saber / Words to Know

(el) nido/ nest

(las) crías/ pups

(la) cola/ tail

Índice / Index